Celebrate the Season!

Celebrate the Season!

Twelve Short Stories for Advent & Christmas

Edited by Diane M. Lynch

BOOKS & MEDIA
Boston

Library of Congress Cataloging-in-Publication Data

Celebrate the season! : twelve short stories for Advent & Christmas / edited by Diane M. Lynch.

   v. cm.

  Summary: A collection of short stories featuring the season that begins with Advent and ends with Epiphany, each followed by "questions to think and talk about."

  Contents: We prepare for Christmas / [by Maria Grace Dateno] -- Katie's Advent countdown / by Teresa Levandoski -- Christmas all year round / by Natacha Sanz-Caballero -- Love forever ; Christmas baby / by Diana R. Jenkins -- Happy Wigilia! / by Barbara Kent Belroy -- A giving heart / by Diana R. Jenkins -- An unexpected gift / by Clare Mishica -- O Holy Night / by Carol A. Grund -- Secret friends / by Diana R. Jenkins -- Lighting up the darkness / by Eugene M. Gagliano -- Thanks a million! / by Diana R. Jenkins -- The day of the Three Kings / by Kathleen M. Muldoon.

  ISBN 0-8198-1585-3 (pbk.)

  1. Christmas stories. 2. Children's stories, American. [1. Short stories. 2. Advent--Fiction. 3. Christmas--Fiction. 4. Epiphany--Fiction.] I. Lynch, Diane M., date.

  PZ5.C2752 2010

  [Fic]--dc22

2009053029

"We Prepare for Christmas" by Maria Grace Dateno, FSP
Cover art by Christian Slade
Design by Mary Joseph Peterson, FSP

Published by Pauline Books & Media, 50 Saint Pauls Avenue, Boston, MA 02130-3491.
www.pauline.org

Printed in the U.S.A.

CTSN VSAUSAPEOILL06-10J10-03254 1585-3

Pauline Books & Media is the publishing house of the Daughters of St. Paul, an international congregation of women religious serving the Church with the communications media.

1 2 3 4 5 6 7 8 9   13 12 11 10

The Catholic Quick Reads Series

Friend 2 Friend

Now You're Cooking!

Family Ties

Goodness Graces!

Celebrate the Season!

Contents

We Prepare for Christmas

Happy New (Church) Year!

When does the new year begin? Well, that depends on your point of view. The new calendar year begins on January 1. Your new school year probably begins in September, or even in August. Spring signals the beginning of a new seasonal year.

In the Catholic Church, the new liturgical (church) year begins on the first Sunday of Advent, which is always four Sundays before Christmas Day. Advent is the season of the Church year that prepares us for Christmas.

And Christmas isn't celebrated only on December 25, either—it's actually a season that lasts about two weeks!

The Church observes some important days during the Advent and Christmas seasons. December 8, the feast of the Immaculate Conception, is a holy day of obligation. The season of Christmas includes two holy days of obligation: Christmas Day itself, and the feast of Mary, the Mother of God. During the Christmas season, we also celebrate several other holy days, including the feast of the Holy Family, Epiphany, and the Baptism of the Lord.

Advent is the season to prepare for the coming of Christ. But exactly what "coming" of Christ are we preparing for? After all, Jesus has already been born in Bethlehem—he was born two thousand years ago. We're not preparing for him to come to the stable. We're preparing for him to come to each of *us*!

The way we do this is by remembering his first coming, as a baby lying in a manger. We think about how so many people, for so

2

long, had been waiting for Jesus to come. God promised to send a Savior, and they trusted him to keep his promise. For many centuries, the Jewish people prayed and prepared for the Messiah. Mary and Joseph did, too. Near the end of Advent, we reflect especially on all the things that happened right before Jesus was born.

Advent happens only once a year, but it's meant to teach us to *always* be expecting Jesus. Jesus "comes" to us every day in many ways! It's a time of waiting, but it's also a time of preparation. Mary didn't just sit around waiting for God's Son to be born. Instead, she looked around to see what needed to be done. She traveled to help her older cousin Elizabeth, who was also expecting a baby. With Elizabeth, she must have washed, mended, cooked, and helped prepare for the birth of that baby—who would grow up to be Saint John the Baptist.

During Advent, when you're waiting for Christmas, look around you. Think about more than just the fun and the presents ahead. Figure

3

out how you can help family members and reach out to neighbors and friends. Then your heart will really be preparing for the coming of Jesus!

The O Antiphons

The final days of Advent are marked with the O Antiphons, short prayer-songs that are recited or chanted during evening prayers. Each antiphon addresses Jesus by a special name or title. We don't know who wrote these beautiful antiphons in Latin sometime between the sixth and ninth centuries, but the verses are full of words and phrases from Scripture.

Here are the beginning lines of the O Antiphons in English:

O Wisdom of God
O Lord and Leader
O Root of Jesse
O Key of David
O Radiant Dawn
O King of All Nations
O Emmanuel

There's something else in the O Antiphons—
a secret message! In Latin, here are the titles for
the Lord in the antiphons:

Sapientia
Adonai
Radix Jesse
Clavis David
Oriens
Rex Gentium
Emmanuel

The first letter of each of these Latin
words, arranged backward, reads "*Ero cras*."
In English, that means "Tomorrow, I will
come!" So, when we sing the final antiphon on
December 23, the message is complete. The
next night will be Christmas Eve, when we
joyously celebrate the coming of Jesus, the Son
of God!

Katie's Advent Countdown

By Teresa Levandoski

"Yesss!" Katie grinned and rushed to her mother's side for a closer look as her mother set the Advent calendar on the dining room table. "Tomorrow's December first! Only twenty-four days until the best day of the year . . . Christmas!"

Every year, Katie's mother would bring the small wooden house down from the attic and fill it with goodies. On the first day of December, Katie would open the first of its many little wooden windows, always curious to discover what type of treat was waiting behind it. Usually it was a piece of candy, but sometimes it would be a clue that would lead her to a small present. She would continue opening one window every day until she opened the last one on Christmas Eve.

The next evening, after dinner, Katie opened the first window. Behind it was a tiny chocolate Christmas wreath. The next day there was a clue to a pair of earrings, and after that, clues to first a bottle of nail polish, then a charm for her bracelet.

Even with the fun of the calendar, time passed much too slowly for Katie, but all that changed on December 15. That day, when Katie reached inside the Advent calendar, she pulled out a piece of purple paper. She read it once and then, puzzled, read it a second time.

"Do something nice for Mrs. Nichols."

Mrs. Nichols? Our neighbor?

"Mom, what's this?"

"Oh, now that you're older, I thought it was time for a few changes."

"But . . ." Katie bit back the rest. *I thought the Advent calendar was supposed to be for me.*

"Looks like you have a job to do. Best get to it."

Turning so her mother couldn't see her face, Katie rolled her eyes and sighed.

Something nice for Mrs. Nichols. The kitchen was still toasty warm and smelled like spices from the gingerbread they had baked earlier in the day. *Gingerbread?* Katie shrugged. *She's old and she lives alone, so she probably doesn't bake much.*

"Do you think she'd like some gingerbread, Mom?"

The big smile on her mother's face was all the answer Katie needed.

Katie knocked on Mrs. Nichols' door and waited, watching the frosty puffs of her breath rise like miniature clouds in the air. A few minutes later, the silver-haired woman peeked from behind the curtain and opened the door. Her wrinkled face softened into a smile of surprise when Katie handed her the plateful of gingerbread squares.

"How wonderful! What a lovely gift! Thank you, Katie."

"You're welcome, Mrs. Nichols. I hope you like it." Katie smiled and turned to leave.

"Oh, come in for just a moment, won't you?" Mrs. Nichols held the door open for Katie. She waited until Katie was inside and then said, "Sit here, I'll be right back."

Katie looked around the small living room. She was surprised to see there was no tree, no stockings, no Advent calendar, no Nativity set, no anything to remind the old woman that Christmas was coming.

When Mrs. Nichols returned, Katie, knowing how sometimes her own grandmother would forget things, said kindly, "You know it's almost Christmas, Mrs. Nichols."

A sad look fell over Mrs. Nichols' face. "Yes, dear, I know."

"But where are your Christmas decorations?"

"Oh, I don't do that anymore. My son and his family live far away now, too far for them to visit, so I gave my decorations to them. There's no point in putting them up just for me." Mrs. Nichols sighed. "Anyhow, I'm too old for all

9

that stuff." She smiled weakly and pressed a wrapped piece of candy into Katie's hand. "Thank you, again."

"Thank you, Mrs. Nichols. Merry Christmas!"

Katie was smiling as she walked home, but she didn't feel completely happy on the inside. Doing something nice for Mrs. Nichols had made her feel good, but she couldn't help feeling a little sad, too.

Later, looking at their brightly lit Christmas tree, Katie got an idea. She went into her bedroom, counted her money, and then went to find her mother.

"Katie, are you sure?" her mother asked when Katie explained what she wanted to buy.

"Please, Mom? I saw the perfect one at the craft store last week. I have enough money. Can we get it tonight? And can we invite Mrs. Nichols for Christmas dinner?"

The very next day, Katie began by painting the sheep. The following evening, she worked on both of the cows. It took two nights to paint all of the shepherds and another two nights to finish the Magi. Then, she began working on Mary, Joseph, and Baby Jesus. Katie painted them very carefully. Finally, it was time for the manger.

"Just in time," Katie said to herself, gently placing the Nativity set into a shiny gold box and covering it with tissue paper. "I can't believe it's already Christmas Eve!"

The next morning Mrs. Nichols came home with them after Mass. Her face lit up when she saw the twinkling, colored lights dancing on the shiny ornaments and the bits of wrapping paper strewn all over the floor.

"Oh, this makes me feel like a little girl again! My family always had a big Christmas celebration. There'd be turkey and stuffing and oh, the presents!" Leaning forward a little, Mrs. Nichols peered closely at the tree. "Why Katie, I think you've forgotten to open one of your presents!"

"Did I?" Katie got up off the floor and walked over to the tree. "Hmmm . . . you're right, there *is* a present here, but the card says that it's for you."

"For me?" Mrs. Nichols' hands shook a little as she took the box from Katie. She read the card, lifted the lid, and pushed aside the green tissue paper.

"Merry Christmas, Mrs. Nichols!"

"Oh, Katie," Mrs. Nichols whispered, "it's beautiful." Holding Mary and Baby Jesus close to her chest with one hand, Mrs. Nichols pulled Katie into a hug with the other. "Thank you. I'll treasure it always."

Katie thought her heart was going to pop. She had never felt as happy as she did right at that moment.

Later, after Mrs. Nichols had gone home, Katie's mother called her into the dining room. "Katie? I think maybe you forgot about something."

"What, Mom?" Katie's eyes followed to where her mother was pointing. "The Advent calendar! I was so busy making Mrs. Nichols' present, I haven't opened a window in days!"

Her mother ruffled Katie's hair and grinned.

Katie sat at the table and opened one of the windows, smiling as she pulled out a little chocolate snowman. As she peeled away its colorful foil wrapper, she was reminded of the happiness on Mrs. Nichols' face as she unwrapped her present. That made Katie's smile grow even bigger. She popped the snowman into her mouth, and as the sweet chocolate melted on her tongue, her head began to fill with ideas of all the wonderful ways she could count down the days until Christmas next year.

Questions to Think and Talk About

Katie's Advent Countdown

1. What's the best Christmas gift you ever received? Who gave it to you? Why was it the best?

2. What's the best Christmas gift you ever gave? What made it so special?

3. How does giving a gift make you feel? What do you get out of it?

4. Does your family have Advent traditions that help you prepare for Christmas? Tell about them.

Christmas All Year Round

By Natacha Sanz-Caballero

"What are you doing?" Kanya asked.

"Huh?" Dylan raised his head. His knuckles were red from the pressure of his chin on them.

"You've been staring at the Nativity scene forever."

"Oh, yeah, I guess," Dylan said as he straightened up. The Harris family always put out the Nativity scene right before Advent started, with Baby Jesus making his appearance on Christmas Eve. Mom thought it was a good way to remind them of what the season was really about, before the Christmas tree became the focal point.

"I was just thinking. Can you imagine what it would have been like to be one of the shepherds?" Dylan asked, his chin back on his knuckles.

Kanya picked up a camel. "If you ask me, I'd rather be one of the kings. Riding on a camel would be cool!"

"Yeah, sure. Anyway, what I mean is, can you imagine following a star to the stable and actually being there when Jesus was born? To really see Jesus with your very own eyes?"

"Yes, I guess. But that happened over two thousand years ago. That was the first Christmas ever, right? So unless you could devise some sort of time machine . . ." said Kanya.

Just then the two heard the garage door opening.

"Hi, Mom. What took you so long?" Kanya asked, running to the door. She picked two grocery bags from her mom's hands and carried them to the kitchen.

"I stopped to visit Mrs. Evans before I went to the market," Mom said, bringing in two more bags from the car.

"Our old neighbor? Isn't she in a nursing home?" Dylan asked, taking the bags to the kitchen.

"That's right." Mom closed the door behind her. "She asked about you two. She sends her love."

"Do you remember Mrs. Evans' orange chocolate chip shortbread cookies?" Dylan asked, as he put a package of vanilla wafers in the pantry.

"They were the best," Kanya added.

"Unfortunately, she can't make them anymore. Her arthritis is preventing her from doing a lot of things she used to do. She can't even knit anymore," Mom said.

"That's too bad," said Kanya, putting some cans of soup in the pantry. "I love the mittens she knitted for me a couple of years ago."

"Leave those cans in the bag, sweetie. And don't empty these two bags either," Mom said, setting them in a corner. "I'm taking them to the Food Bank."

"Hi, guys. How was everybody's day?" Dad asked as he walked in. He put his briefcase down and hung up his jacket. "Oh, I love Fridays!"

"Today we . . ." Dylan started. The phone rang. Kanya picked it up.

"Dad, it's for you. It's Mrs. Potchka from next door."

"Hi, Sally. Yes . . . No problem at all . . . I'll be glad to. Let me talk to Lauren and see how our schedule looks for tomorrow. I'll call you right back."

Mom was busy preparing dinner.

"Sally Potchka was wondering if I could help her hang her outdoor Christmas lights. Her son used to wrap some around the blue spruce, but she can't reach."

"Oh, sure. No problem," Mom said. A carrot rolled off the counter. Dad caught it midair and started munching. "Tomorrow morning will be a good time for that," she continued. "Kanya, Dylan, and I can go to the Food Bank while you're there."

"But Mom—weren't we going to shop for my new basketball shoes?" Dylan complained.

"Tomorrow's Saturday, Dylan. There'll be time for everything," Mom said, emptying a bag of noodles into the boiling water. "It's very difficult for Mrs. Potchka since her son moved away, and we're glad to give her a hand."

"You're right. Sorry," Dylan said.

"You know what, Dylan? Maybe you can help me tomorrow with those lights," Dad said, pouring himself a glass of soda. "When we finish we can go get you those shoes."

"And then we can all meet at Phil's Pizza for lunch," Mom added.

"That sounds great," Dylan said.

❄   ❄   ❄

The lights looked pretty in Mrs. Potchka's yard. They even placed one shaped like a star on top of the blue spruce.

"It reminds me of the star of Bethlehem," Dylan said.

"That must have been quite a bright star," Dad said, looking up at the tree.

"I wonder what it would have been like to follow that star," Dylan said. "Can you imagine seeing Jesus with your very own eyes? To be there on the first Christmas ever?"

Dad started to pick up his tools. "I guess we'd be celebrities now!" he joked. "We'd be included in every Nativity scene in the world!"

"Dad!"

"Sorry, son. Seriously, it would have been quite amazing."

Mrs. Potchka walked out. She was carrying a cookie tin.

"Thanks so much for your help. The lights look terrific. Please take these cookies with you," she said, handing Dylan the tin. "Say hi to your mom for me, will you?"

"I will. Thank you, Mrs. Potchka."

❄ ❄ ❄

Phil's Pizza was delicious, as always. And the new basketball shoes were cool.

The cookie tin was still on the kitchen counter when they got home.

"Mrs. Potchka gave us some cookies. Can we have one?" asked Dylan, as he started opening the tin. "Hey, don't these look like Mrs. Evans' orange chocolate chip shortbread cookies?"

"You're right," Mom said, grabbing one. "Hmm, and they taste like Mrs. Evans', too."

Mom picked up the phone and dialed.

"Sally? Hi, it's Lauren. I was calling to thank you for the cookies . . . Yes, I noticed . . . Really? She gave you the recipe? Is that right? Well, that's a very nice thing to do . . . a lot of people will need those this winter . . . You too; enjoy the rest of the weekend."

"You were right, Dylan. That was Mrs. Evans' cookie recipe," Mom said after hanging up the phone. "Mrs. Potchka visited her a few days ago at the nursing home and they struck a deal."

"What kind of deal?" Dylan asked.

"Mrs. Evans asked Mrs. Potchka to knit three scarves and three hats to bring to the City Shelter," Mom said. "She had been doing it for years, but with her arthritis, she couldn't do it anymore. In exchange, she gave Mrs. Potchka her special recipe."

"It's like a tradition has been passed on," Kanya added.

"That's a good way to put it," Mom said.

The following night at the dinner table, Mom lit the first candle in their Advent wreath.

"You know what?" Dylan said, after the family had blessed the meal. "I think maybe we do know what it would have been like to see Jesus."

"Really? How?" Kanya asked.

"Well, when we act the way he would— by being kind to each other and helpful and generous with people who need us—it's almost like he really is here. That's what I think, anyway."

"I never thought of it like that," Kanya said.

"Good job, Dylan! And," Dad said, "the good news is we can do that all year round, and not just at Christmas time."

That night Mom looked for her knitting needles.

"Can you teach me how to knit, Mom?" Kanya asked. "Maybe by next Christmas I'll know how to make hats and scarves."

Mom smiled. "Let's get going, then."

Advent was off to a great start!

Questions to Think and Talk About

Christmas
All Year Round

1. Generosity of heart means putting other people's needs before your own. Was there a time when you put off something you really wanted to do—and instead did something for somebody else? How did it make you feel?

2. Can you think of three things you could do to be generous of heart during Advent?

3. How about three things you can do to be generous of heart during the rest of the year?

4. Does your school or parish hold an Advent activity that you enjoy? What makes it special?

Love Forever

By Diana R. Jenkins

I'll just be up front right now: I tried to
manipulate my little sister. It sounds terrible,
but I was tired of getting stuff like gargantuan
tubs of bubble gum bubble bath. For once, I
wanted a good Christmas gift!

One afternoon when we were in our
bedroom, I turned on the radio and put my
plan into action. I had to wait awhile, but
finally "Love Forever" came on. I turned up the
radio and said, "Hey, Elena, do you like this
song?"

She came over by my bed and listened. "Yeah, I do, Isabel," she said, bouncing her head in time to the music.

"That song's called 'Love Forever,'" I told her. "And the CD is called *Love Forever*, too. It's by the Amber Daisies."

"I like it," said Elena.

"I'd play it all the time if I had the CD," I hinted.

"Maybe someone will give it to you for Christmas," she said with a smile.

I smiled back. "Yeah, maybe." *That was easy!* I thought.

The next day, Elena was supposed to go to the mall with Mom. While she was in our room getting ready, I decided to make sure that she'd gotten my hint before. "Are you Christmas shopping today?" I asked.

"Maybe," she said.

"I love finding the right Christmas gift for somebody," I said. "You know, something that they really want?"

"Mm-hmm," she said. "See you later, Isabel!"

"Wait, Elena," I said. "Do you remember the name of that song we listened to yesterday?"

"Of course!" she said. "Bye!"

I felt confident that my plan had worked—until Elena and Mom got back home. Mom opened all the shopping bags that they'd carried into the house and showed me everything she'd bought.

"Now I have all my gifts," said Mom.

"Didn't you do any shopping, Elena?" I asked.

"No," she said. "I don't know what to get anybody."

"What!" I cried. Mom looked at me funny, so I added, "I'm sure you'll think of some great ideas."

Maybe, I thought, *I should just tell Elena to buy the CD.* But I knew Mom would be mad if she found out. She doesn't allow us to ask for things or make lists. She has this idea that people should come up with what she calls "gifts from the heart." That sounds nice, but she'd feel differently if she'd ever bathed in bubble gum bubbles!

I tried to think how I could get Elena to give me that CD—from her heart, of course! One night I had youth group while Elena had choir practice. As I walked her toward the practice room, I hummed "Love Forever." When we reached the door, I said, "That's really a pretty song, isn't it?"

"Yes, it is!" said Elena. "I just love Christmas music."

"That wasn't a Christmas song," I said.

"That wasn't 'Silent Night'?"

"No," I said. "That was 'Love Forever.' You know, that song we listened to on the radio? The one from the CD by the Amber Daisies?"

"Oh," she said. "Maybe it's a good thing you're not in the choir, Isabel. See you later!"

After shopping one Saturday, I "let" Elena help me wrap gifts. As we worked, I continued with my Christmas plot. "That was easy," I said after we finished wrapping a book for Grandma.

"Yep," said Elena. "What's next?"

"Have you ever noticed how easy it is to wrap things with straight sides?" I said.

"No," she said.

"Well, it is," I said. "Like it was hard to wrap Francie's stuffed bear, but the book was so simple. Do you know what the easiest thing to wrap is?"

"Books?" said Elena.

"No," I said. "CDs! They're so easy to wrap. And they make fantastic gifts. I love CDs."

"Me, too," said Elena.

"I especially like 'Love Forever,'" I said. "I really like it. Know what I mean?"

Elena smiled. "I know what you mean."

I would have said more, but Mom came in to wrap her gifts with us. As soon as she sat down, Elena said, "Do you know what's the easiest thing to wrap, Mom?"

"Well, it's not the cookie jar I made for Aunt Marta!" she said, holding up the bear-shaped jar.

"Here, let me help you, Mom," I said quickly. "Why don't you wrap that scarf, Elena?"

Fortunately, Elena got busy and quit talking!

Over the next few days, I tried dropping a few other hints, but I was afraid to say too much. I didn't want Elena to blab something incriminating to Mom!

When Elena handed me her gift on Christmas morning, my first thought was, *Yes!* The small, square package looked just like a CD! But when I opened it, I saw that Elena had painted me a small, square picture on a thick piece of cardboard.

"See, Isabel?" she said, pointing to the picture. "See how the rainbow leads to a heart instead of a pot of gold?"

"Yeah, I see," I said dully. Mom frowned, so I added, "Thanks, Elena."

When I took my gifts to my room later, I thought about just throwing away Elena's stupid painting. Of course, I couldn't do that. I'd have to display it for a while at least. *Sheesh!* I thought as I set the picture up on my dresser. *This is even worse than the stuff she usually gives me!*

"Isn't it cool?" Elena was standing in the doorway, looking proud.

"Right," I said.

"It's a gift from the heart," she said.

"How sweet," I muttered.

"Mom always says we should give something from the heart," she went on. "That's what Christmas is for. Giving!"

How about giving me a break? I thought.

"Because God gave us the best gift of all," she said. "His only Son. That really was a gift from the heart, wasn't it?"

For a minute I couldn't say anything. I couldn't even look at Elena. I just stood there, staring at her painting and feeling stupid. And selfish! I'd been acting like I didn't even know what Christmas was about, and Elena . . . well, Elena had a heart as big as the one she'd painted at the end of the rainbow!

"You know what?" I said after I swallowed the big lump in my throat. "I think this is the best gift I ever got."

"It is?" said Elena.

"You bet!" I said.

"Did you read what I wrote on the back of the picture?" she asked, bouncing up and down a little.

I turned the painting over. Can you guess what I read there?

That's right.

"Love forever."

Questions to Think and Talk About

Love Forever

1. Why is it wrong to manipulate others?

2. What gifts from the heart have you received? What gifts have you given from the heart?

3. Isabel's family had a tradition of not asking for particular gifts. What Christmas traditions does your family have?

4. Sometimes we forget that Christmas is about God's wonderful gift of his Son. What are some things we can do to keep focused on Jesus during the season?

Christmas Baby

By Diana R. Jenkins

Maybe this sounds dumb, but I couldn't wait to be a big brother. Being an only child is pretty boring, so I was actually happy that Mom was going to have a baby. I even thought it was lucky the baby would be born at Christmastime. Becoming a big brother was going to be one of the best things that had ever happened to me.

Or so I thought!

"Listen, Austin," Mom told me one day. "Taking care of a baby is not easy."

"I know," I said. Which I really didn't, but I didn't know that then.

"So here are some books to help you learn about it."

"Thanks, Mom!" I'm into reading, so I was eager to dive into the stack of books she gave me.

Some of the babies in the books looked like they were laughing. Some of them had goofy expressions that made me laugh. Some were sleeping, some were pouting, and some were wearing weird hats. But they all looked cute. So I figured my baby brother or sister would be, too. I mean . . . the books made it seem like a sure thing.

I read all the chapters that were about taking care of a baby. It sounded like a lot of fun. I studied about how to hold, bathe, feed, and diaper babies, since soon I'd be doing those things with my own cute little sister or brother. By the time I was finished with the books, I felt like a real expert.

The last day before Christmas vacation, Dad picked me up at school with the news that the baby had been born! It was a boy! I asked Dad to take me right to the hospital to see my new baby brother. But as he drove off, I said, "Wait! Do you have the camera?"

"It's in the trunk," he said.

"Good," I told him. "Let's take lots of pictures, okay?"

But when we got to Mom's room and I actually saw the baby, I got the shock of my life. His face was scrunched up into this mean expression, he didn't have any hair, and his head was lopsided! Dad took a lot of photos like I'd asked, but I had to wonder why. I mean . . . that kid didn't look like any of the cute babies in the books!

"We're naming him 'Beau,'" said Dad proudly.

"It means 'handsome,'" said Mom, kissing the baby's splotchy forehead.

"Cool!" I said. But inside I was thinking that was the last name I would have called him! *Come on. Let's get real.*

When Mom and Beau came home from the hospital, I found out that a real, live baby is nothing like a baby in a book. Something gross was always coming out of Beau somewhere. He was way heavier to hold than I had imagined. And he cried all the time!

And remember how lucky I thought it was that he was going to be a Christmas baby? Ha! Beau couldn't even talk, but right away he started wrecking my whole Christmas vacation. And I could see that Christmas itself was going to be ruined, too!

Mom and Dad were so busy with Beau that I had to decorate the Christmas tree by myself. Gee, how fun! I tried singing some Christmas carols like we usually do while we're trimming the tree, but I sounded lame all by myself. And when Beau started crying in the other room and drowned out my voice, I just gave up. I slapped the rest of the ornaments on the tree, threw on a few wads of tinsel, and left the star there for Dad to put on the top later.

On another day, I asked Mom for wrapping paper for the presents I was giving. She was trying to give Beau a bottle, but he wouldn't stop crying long enough for her to get it into his mouth. "We don't have any wrapping paper!" she yelled over him. "You'll have to use newspapers!"

I did what she said, but my presents didn't look Christmassy at all. And after I put them under the tree, they sat there all by themselves. For days! Not even one other gift appeared!

When I said, "Looks kind of empty under the tree." Dad said, "You already got a big gift, Austin." I realized that he meant my little brother. I hoped that Beau wasn't going to be my only present!

We didn't go caroling with our church group or decorate cookies or help with the annual food drive. All we did was take care of Beau and listen to him cry. Being a big brother was terrible!

At least we did go to our church's Christmas pageant. The baby they had to play Jesus was really cute, but I wasn't impressed. Now I knew what a pain babies could be!

The shepherds had just arrived when "Baby Jesus" started wailing. He was so loud you couldn't hear the shepherds' lines.

Then Beau started crying, too!

Then another baby started in. And another. And another.

Pretty soon, they had to stop the play because of the noise! Some people laughed, but I just thought it was annoying.

The girl who was playing Mary picked up "Baby Jesus" and rocked him. She did a good job, holding him just like it showed in the baby books. Of course, the real Mary didn't have any baby books to help her know how to do things.

But, the thought hit me, *the real Mary had . . . a real baby!* I guess I never thought about that much before. In pictures, Baby Jesus always looks so holy and sweet—and quiet!

I looked at Beau screaming in Mom's arms and thought, *Jesus was a baby like that! A helpless little baby! God sent his Son to us as a baby! What an amazing gift!*

Then I got another incredible thought: *If Jesus was like the babies in this church, then aren't the babies in this church like Jesus? Maybe God sends us babies as a gift to remind us of Jesus—the best gift ever!*

Beau's face was all wrinkled up and his nose was running and he was wailing his head off, but he was a gift from God. Especially for me and my family! Don't get me wrong: I didn't suddenly feel like taking care of a baby was great fun or anything. But I did feel more grateful for the chance to be a big brother.

I took out a tissue and wiped Beau's nose. Then I said to Mom, "Maybe I can quiet him down." Mom looked at Dad and then set Beau in my arms. He stared up at me silently for a moment and then he smiled right at me! It was like he understood I was his brother.

As the pageant went on, I said a little prayer, thanking God for all his gifts. And when Beau starting shrieking again, I prayed for God's help to be a good brother. And, I have to admit, I asked that a certain present would turn up under our Christmas tree.

Earplugs!

Questions to Think and Talk About

Christmas Baby

1. Austin found out that reading about something can be very different from living it. Tell about a time you felt the same way.

2. What's the biggest change your family has experienced? How did everyone adjust to it?

3. Something that seems like a problem can turn out to be a blessing from God. What's the good side of a troublesome situation in your life?

4. Christmas activities are more meaningful when other people are involved. How do you share Christmas with your family and friends?

Happy *Wigilia!*

By Barbara Kent Belroy

In December 1985, the year I turned twelve, I was freaking out because my aunt, uncle, and cousins were coming for Christmas—all the way from Poland! My uncle got an engineering job here, and they'd be living with us until they found a house, which meant I'd have to share my room with my cousin Krysia, who was twelve, like me. I was an only child, and now I'd have to give up my privacy. Her twin brothers were four, so they'd probably be a pain in the neck.

The night before they came, I couldn't sleep, but I finally did, and when I woke up, I heard strange voices downstairs. I grabbed my robe and raced down to the kitchen.

Five brand-new people sat at the breakfast table. The grown-ups drank tea. One twin sat in his mom's lap, his thumb in his mouth. The other sat at the table, eating one of Mom's homemade snickerdoodles. Krysia was standing by her father.

Mom and Daddy introduced us. Uncle Antoni and Aunt Zosia had accents like my parents. At least they spoke English. I wasn't sure about my cousins, but when we shook hands, all three whispered, "Nice to meet you, Basia." A good sign, I guess.

"Well, let's take you to your rooms," Daddy said. I carried some of their small bags. My parents put my uncle and aunt in the guest room and Jurek and Stefan in Daddy's office, which was now fixed up with bunk beds. My parents said the twins would take the beds when they moved to their own house eventually. I wondered when that would be.

Finally, we went to my room to drop off Krysia's small suitcase. It was official. I no longer had my own room.

After dinner, we bought a Christmas tree. Usually, I got to decorate it myself. I'd probably have to let one of my "guests" put the star up now, just to be polite.

After Daddy put on the bubble lights, we all decorated the tree, working together to place the ornaments in just the right spots. Jurek put a Santa ornament way at the bottom. Krysia and I glanced at one another, and when Jurek wasn't looking, we laughed as we both rushed to rescue it, placing it higher.

"Who wants to put the star on top?" I asked. My cousins shrugged. "C'mon," I said, "aren't we going to argue over it or something?"

"You do it," Krysia said.

I climbed the ladder and placed the star at the tip of the tree.

When we turned on the lights, my cousins looked really happy. Then we set up the Nativity scene, keeping Baby Jesus wrapped away in a box for Christmas morning.

In bed that night, I thought Krysia would want to talk, but she fell asleep right away.

The next day our house was filled with yummy smells. Mom and Aunt Zosia rolled dough to make *pierogies*, a kind of potato-and-onion-filled pocket. Krysia and I helped fill the pockets. I was kind of slow and clumsy, but she wrapped them fast. Hers were perfect. Mine were lumpy.

We were still going to have our usual Christmas turkey dinner with all the trimmings, but Mom wanted this to be a Polish Christmas Eve, or *Wigilia*, as she called it (pronounced "ve-GEEL-ya"). She and Aunt Zosia also made beet soup, cabbage rolls, poppy-seed strudel, and fruitcake. My parents came to the United States in their twenties, and I was born here, so I was used to American food. This was going to be different. Lumpy and different.

The next day would be Christmas Eve. I was looking forward to opening my presents Christmas morning, even though my parents got me less stuff because they were buying for four kids, instead of just me. In bed that night, Krysia and I lay quietly.

"Are you going to move to a house soon?" I asked her. I wanted to know how long I'd have to share my space.

"I don't know."

"Do you like our house? It's big, huh?"

"Yes, very big."

"You probably didn't have a house this big," I said.

"We lived in a one-bedroom apartment."

"One bedroom?!" I sat up. "With five of you? How could you all fit? Didn't you even have your own room?"

"Of course not. I shared a room with my brothers. Mama and Papa slept in the living room—on a sofa that opened into a bed."

"Wow!" I turned on the light. "You didn't have your own room? What about a bathroom?" I couldn't imagine sharing my bathroom. I had everything in the right place.

"The bathroom was shared by all families living on the same apartment floor," Krysia said.

"No way!!!"

"Yes, way!!" she laughed. Then she got serious. "It's very hard to find a house in

Poland. People have to sometimes wait fifteen years."

"You're kidding! Wasn't it awful sharing with your brothers?"

"It was difficult. But it was fun, too! When we had chicken pox, we told funny stories and laughed all night. Mama yelled, 'Go to sleep. You're supposed to be sick.' This just made us laugh even more."

I thought about when I'd had chicken pox alone. I'd watched television and almost died of itchy boredom. It had been kind of fun decorating the tree together last night. But still, my space was being invaded, and I hoped they'd find a house soon. At least it wouldn't take fifteen years here!

The next day, on Christmas Eve, Krysia ran to the table and put some shredded brown paper in a bowl, covering it with a white napkin.

"What's that?" I asked.

"It's the hay and the manger, Christ's crib. It's a Polish tradition." Then she ran to the dining room door and opened it slightly before coming back to the table. "We have to set another table setting and leave the door open in case of an extra guest. Another Polish tradition."

Daddy explained that the "extra guest" also represented Jesus. I was just surprised that anyone who had lived in such a small, crowded apartment, like Krysia had, would even think about opening the door to more people.

At the dinner table before eating, Aunt Zosia brought out what looked like rectangular communion wafers, only they weren't consecrated. She called them *opłatek* (pronounced oh-PWAH-tek). They were shaped like little cards and had the Nativity scene etched into them. They were so cool! We broke off little pieces and exchanged them, telling one another nice things, like "Merry Christmas. May God bless you in the new year," or "May you have health and good grades." Then we'd hug and kiss and eat the small piece of *opłatek*.

This went on until almost everyone had greeted one another. Suddenly Krysia came up to me. She broke off a piece of her *opłatek* and, handing it to me, she said, "May we become close, like sisters. And thank you for sharing your room. I know it must be very difficult for you." She hugged me.

Then I broke off a piece of my *opłatek* and handed it to her.

"And may you not find a house—" I said, "at least, not right away."

Questions to Think and Talk About

Happy *Wigilia!*

1. Do you think Basia is used to having her own way? What tells you that?

2. At what point in the story do you sense that Basia is starting to think that sharing might be a good thing?

3. Have you ever had to share something that was important to you? Tell what that was like.

4. Why does Basia tell Krysia, "And may you not find a house—at least, not right away"?

A Giving Heart

By Diana R. Jenkins

"Miguel!"

Uncle Carlos pushed through the crowd and hugged me. "Are you all right?" he asked. When I nodded, he hugged Mama and my little brother, Diego. "Thank God you're all okay!"

"We are truly blessed," said Mama.

Blessed? Our apartment building was totally destroyed! I was glad that no one had been hurt in the fire, but I sure didn't feel "blessed."

"What a shame!" said Uncle Carlos, looking at the black, smoky mess that used to be our home. "Right before Christmas!"

I thought about our beautiful Christmas tree, our special clay Nativity set from Mexico, and, most of all, our gifts. What a terrible Christmas we were going to have!

Uncle Carlos drove us to his tiny apartment and made cheeseburgers. I hadn't had any supper, but I couldn't eat much anyway. Afterward, we all went to bed—if you can call it that! Mama and Diego slept on the sofa bed while Uncle Carlos and I slept on some blankets on the hard floor. I was awake most of the night!

The next morning, Uncle Carlos left us his car keys when he went to work. I didn't have to go to school. Instead, Mama drove us to the church, and we went to the Neighbor to Neighbor room.

The lady there told us how sorry she was about the fire. "Take anything you need," she said.

I went to the table of boys' clothes. Everything looked like something my grandfather would wear! It was all so out of style. And used!

Sadly, I thought of my favorite clothes, now burned to ashes.

"There's nothing here," I told Mama.

"Let me help you." She dug around and found some shirts and pants in my size. "There! That'll hold you awhile." She seemed happy so I didn't say anything about how awful the clothes looked.

Later Mama took us to the restaurant to tell her boss she'd be back to work as soon as possible.

"Don't worry about it," he said. Then he told us to have lunch on the house—which meant we didn't have to pay.

"God bless you," said Mama.

"Thanks!" said Diego.

I felt totally embarrassed. Like we were some kind of charity case!

That afternoon, Uncle Carlos came home with a toy car for Diego and a book for me. I thanked him and pretended to read. Really I was thinking about all the books I used to have. Now all I had was one! One!

The next day, Mama insisted I go to school so I wouldn't miss the Christmas party. Everyone there acted nice and said they were sorry about the fire, but I could tell they were looking at my dweeby clothes.

When we went to the church to rehearse our Christmas Day program, I felt like hiding. We each had to get up in front of everyone and say why we were offering our gift, then place it near the Nativity scene. Later our gifts would be given to needy kids.

I knew what everyone was thinking: *Needy kids! Like Miguel!*

Luckily our gifts for the program were in our desks at school, or I would have had nothing to offer Baby Jesus. My gift was a set of colored pencils. I had planned to say that I was giving them because I was thankful for the gift of art, but that seemed so lame now. Who cared about art when everything I owned was burnt to a crisp?

I got through the rehearsal with a flaming red face and an angry heart. Then we went back to our classroom, and everybody got out their presents for our gift exchange. Everybody except me. The cool game I'd bought for the exchange had gone up in smoke with the rest of my life!

"Don't worry, Miguel," Mrs. Patrice told me. "I brought an extra gift."

She said it quietly, but I figured everybody knew anyway. They were probably feeling sorry for me because I didn't have anything to give. How embarrassing!

I was so glad when that day was over, but the next few days weren't so great either. I had to babysit Diego while Mama went to work. We really needed the money! But being stuck in Uncle Carlos' tiny apartment all day with my little brother wasn't much of a vacation.

Mostly we watched Uncle Carlos' old television. The holiday programs made me feel terrible. My Christmas was ruined! Hey, my life was ruined!

On Christmas morning, we put on our "best" used clothes, and Uncle Carlos drove us to church. My class sat together holding our gifts because we were doing our program first.

Before we started, Reverend Nuncio talked about how Christmas is about giving. I didn't really much listen until he said, "The shepherds were poor, but they gave what they could. And their love meant as much as the riches of kings. You see," he smiled warmly, "it's the giving that matters—not the gift itself."

That made me think of Uncle Carlos helping us, even though he didn't have much money. Then I thought of the donated clothes in the Neighbor to Neighbor room. And the free meal from Mama's boss. And Mrs. Patrice's gift. So many people had been giving to my family!

And Mama . . . she was always giving, giving to me and Diego.

I looked at the manger, which now held the statue of Baby Jesus. God had given his own Son. What an amazing act of giving that had been!

I felt kind of ashamed. I had only been thinking of me, me, me! Where was my giving spirit?

Right then I decided to change my attitude—to think about what I had to give instead of worrying about what I didn't have! Somehow, I had to be more giving. There were all kinds of ways I could do that. And I knew just how to begin.

I still felt funny about my used clothes, but getting up in front of everyone was different this time. I said my words like I meant them— which I did! And I offered my gift with my heart.

With a giving heart.

Questions to Think and Talk About

A Giving Heart

1. Why did Miguel's mother feel they were blessed?

2. Who has been "giving" to you in times of trouble?

3. Jesus is God's greatest gift to us, but he has filled our lives with many other blessings, too. Which of God's gifts could you appreciate more?

4. Have you ever had trouble accepting help from others? How did you deal with the situation?

An Unexpected Gift

By Clare Mishica

"Jessica!" my mom called up. "Time to go."

"Coming!" I hollered, launching myself off my bed and racing down the steps. This year I was in our Christmas pageant, and today we had our dress rehearsal.

"Me comin'," announced my three-year-old sister, Kiana, as I grabbed my jacket from the closet. She had my mom's hat on backward, and her raggedy old blanket was wrapped around her like a cape.

"She's coming?" I asked Mom. I loved Kiana, but she can be lots of work. The day before, she'd stuck a whole package of bendy straws to the television with our Christmas stickers. It looked like an alien.

"Your dad's working an extra shift," Mom explained, tugging on Kiana's coat. "Kiana will sit and watch your practice."

I thought there was a much better chance that Kiana would knock over the stable.

"Let's go," Mom said, grabbing Kiana's hand and holding open the door. "I promised Mrs. Hoff I'd help with the costumes."

"Okay," I sighed as Kiana dragged her blanket behind her in the snow. That old thing is more attached to my sister than her arms and legs.

When we walked into the church hall, it sounded a little like the playground at recess time. Kids from grades one to six were running all over the place.

"Attention!" Mrs. Hoff called out. Her voice is sharper than a whistle, and everyone froze.

"Jessica's mom will help you get your costumes," Mrs. Hoff said next. "Please get in line."

Everyone bumped and pushed, and Chazz Wilson stomped on my foot.

"Sorry," he mumbled, but my toe still hurt enough to make my eyes water.

"Jessica, take Kiana for a minute," Mom said. "I'll get your costume when I'm done with the others."

"Come on, Kiana," I grumbled. When Mom had first told me she was helping with the pageant, I thought I might get a little special treatment. I did—I was last for everything.

I took Kiana to see our stable, but she wanted to climb in the manger.

"Me sleep," she said.

"No way, Kiana," I scolded. "Just stay out of trouble for two minutes."

Kiana stared at me and her smile melted away. "Me want Mama," she said.

"Me, too," I complained as a wave of frustration washed over me. Nothing seemed to go the way I planned. I didn't want my dad working extra hours. I didn't want to help watch Kiana, and when my mom handed me the scratchy brown costume, I didn't want to be a shepherd.

Mrs. Hoff started playing the first song, and Mary and Joseph walked down the aisle. A second later, Joseph tripped over his robe and knocked Mary into the donkey. I'm sure our Mary yells a lot louder than the real Mary ever did.

"Patience, everyone," said Mrs. Hoff. "Let's try again."

I watched from the back hall with the three kings. They were all wearing long, silky gowns with glittering turbans and crowns. They also got to carry shiny silver boxes with their gifts for Baby Jesus. I got to carry my grandpa's old wooden cane; I'd probably get slivers.

This time, Mary and Joseph made it to the first inn, but the innkeeper forgot his only line.

"The inn is full; we have no room," whispered the donkey, and everyone giggled.

I think Mrs. Hoff was getting frustrated, too, because her voice sounded stretched and tight like a rubber band. She had to tell the angels where to stand three times in a row, and then one of them had to go to the bathroom. It must have been contagious, because pretty soon Joseph and the donkey had to go, too.

Finally, it was the shepherd's turn. I walked toward the stage with my sheep, Billy, Sofia, and Fabio, but no one listened to me. Billy kept pulling his ears off, and Sofia waved to everyone as if she was a movie star parading down the red carpet.

"Stop waving," I whispered loudly.

A moment later, Joseph came hurrying back, but he tripped over Mary's long robe and crashed against the stable wall. The whole cardboard stable tumbled down like a house of cards.

"Oh, my!" cried Mrs. Hoff, and everyone scrambled onto the stage at once.

"Look what you did," the innkeeper muttered to Joseph. "Now our walls are ripped."

"It was an accident," the angel argued. "At least he remembers his line."

"Yeah, well, I don't have to run to the bathroom when I'm nervous," snapped the innkeeper.

Suddenly, Mary hollered loud enough for the real angels to hear. "The Baby Jesus doll is missing!" she cried.

Everyone stopped talking, and Mrs. Hoff took advantage of that sudden quiet break.

"Calm down," she told us. "We'll fix the stable and find Jesus. I'm sure he didn't just disappear."

"Baby Jesus cold," Kiana piped up, and everyone turned to look at her. She was standing behind one of my sheep, and she'd wrapped Jesus in her old raggedy blanket.

"Jesus sleep with my night-night," Kiana said, and then she walked over and straightened out the manger. Gently, she put Jesus back to bed, tucking the blanket around him. Then she bent down and kissed his cheek.

"Kiana, you're very kind," said Mrs. Hoff, and, at that instant, something in the room changed.

Kiana had reminded us that Jesus is about loving. He's about loving others enough to let go of your favorite blanket, so you can wrap your caring right around them.

Almost like magic, the innkeeper and Joseph started fixing the stable together, and I helped Billy with his sheep ears. Later, as the angels sang their song again, I stared at Jesus as he slept beneath Kiana's raggedy blue blanket. I thought about the long hours that my dad worked to help our family out and about how often Mom volunteered. Maybe Kiana and I could make them some surprise thank-you cards and put them under their pillows. They'd really like that . . .

The angels finished their song, and I walked with my sheep toward the manger. My costume still made my arms and legs itch, but it didn't matter. Inside, I felt a warm Christmas glow that made me grin. It had been tucked inside that old raggedy blue blanket . . . along with Baby Jesus.

Questions to Think and Talk About

An Unexpected Gift

1. Describe Jessica's feelings when she discovers her sister Kiana is coming along. Have you ever had similar feelings? How did you deal with them?

2. Jessica thinks she should receive "special treatment" because her mother is helping with the pageant. Have you ever been expected to do more than your share in a certain situation? How did you feel?

3. Is your viewpoint influenced when you spend time with someone who is angry or unhappy? What can you do to change that situation?

4. Why is Kiana's gift a true gift of the heart? What's the most touching gift you've ever received? What's the most loving gift you've given?

O Holy Night

By Carol A. Grund

The voices in Nathan's dream urged him to hurry.

"Go!" they cried, as he flew across the ice—faster, faster!—his stick guiding the puck straight toward the net like a heat-seeking missile. The fans kept chanting his name and stomping their feet. As the pounding grew louder, their voices seemed to merge into one voice.

"Nathan! It's time to go! Mom says you've already missed breakfast, and we're leaving in fifteen minutes!"

Nathan groaned and rolled over. His dream of hockey glory had turned into the nightmare of his little sister pounding on the bedroom door.

"Knock it off, Molly!" he told her. "I'm coming!"

"Okay, but the roads are slippery, so you have to hurry."

Struggling out from under his heavy blankets, Nathan stumbled to the window. The world outside was transformed. A fresh layer of snow sparkled on every surface, just in time for a white Christmas tomorrow.

Christmas. The week leading up to it was one of the best weeks of the year. No school meant no homework, no bus, no morning alarm clock. Best of all, it meant plenty of time to hang out at the rink, playing pickup hockey with his friends.

At least, that's what it **usually** meant. But a few days ago, his mother had busted those plans all to pieces.

"I told Mrs. Paulsen, the choir director, that you'd help out at the Christmas Eve Mass," she'd said a few days ago. "She's putting together a group of middle school students to accompany the children's choir, and I told her you would play your clarinet."

Nathan had felt as stunned as if a puck had just caught him in the chest. This new scenario had so many things wrong with it, his brain couldn't pick one to settle on.

For one thing, that Christmas Eve Mass stuff was for little kids. He used to dress up like a shepherd and join in the processional, but that was back in grade school. These days he preferred a nice anonymous pew somewhere in the back.

And his clarinet? Ever since he'd hurt his wrist at hockey camp last summer, he'd barely had the thing out of its case. How could anyone expect him to be playing Christmas carols in only a few days?

Worst of all, he could see his plans for hanging out at the rink melting into a big sloppy pile of slush. But no matter how much he protested, his mom wouldn't budge.

"Mrs. Paulsen needs help, and she's counting on you. Molly's going to be in the processional—this way you can participate, too."

So far he'd dragged himself out of a warm bed to "participate" in two rehearsals. Only six other kids had shown up. They were all from another school except for Lauren, who had been in Nathan's band class last year. He'd barely spoken ten words to her then, but in this awkward situation, they'd latched on to each other like long-lost friends. Or, it occurred to Nathan, like rats on a sinking ship.

"Hi," Lauren said today, as he gulped down his last bite of a breakfast bar. It was all he'd had time to grab on his way out the door. "Ready for our big debut tonight?"

Nathan snorted. "Ready for it to be over, if that's what you mean."

"Yeah, I guess we *are* pretty terrible," Lauren said. "It's hard for a group that's never played together before. And Mrs. Paulsen is really a choir teacher, not a band leader."

"John Philip Sousa couldn't lead this band," Nathan pointed out. "We squeak and squawk more than a barnyard full of chickens."

Lauren grinned as she started assembling her flute. "Maybe the choir will drown us out."

"Or maybe it will snow six more feet and they'll have to cancel the whole thing," he said. "But don't count on it—I'm never that lucky."

Mrs. Paulsen had been busy arranging choir members on the other side of the altar. Now she stood in the center to address both groups.

"As you know, this is our last chance to polish our performance," she said. "The entrance hymn will be sung without instruments, so let's skip that for now and practice the songs the band will join us on. Is everyone ready?"

Nathan was pretty sure Mrs. Paulsen wouldn't appreciate his honest answer to that question. But he couldn't resist turning to Lauren to whisper, "In other words, let the squawking begin."

❄   ❄   ❄

Hours later, Nathan was back in his folding chair beside the altar, this time dressed in his

Sunday best. He'd thought rehearsals were bad, but now that the church was filling up with people waiting for a performance he knew would be a disaster, he'd actually begun wishing a hole would appear in the floor, a hole big enough to swallow him until the whole thing was over.

Finally the pews were filled. Someone turned down the overhead lights, and, as if on cue, the crowd hushed. Nathan was surprised to feel a shiver run through him as he looked around the now silent church, filled with evergreen boughs and lit by soft, flickering candlelight. Then Mrs. Paulsen raised her arms, and the choir began singing "Silent Night" in their clear, young voices.

From the back of the church, a line of children dressed as angels and shepherds moved slowly up the aisle, almost floating in the dim light. Nathan spotted Molly, wearing Mom's old robe and a tinsel halo. He thought she really did look angelic—practically a miracle in itself.

With the children gathered on the altar, Mrs. Paulsen cued the band. Nathan took a deep breath, raised his clarinet, and began to play, his notes blending with the other instruments and the choir.

> O Holy Night! The stars are brightly shining;
> It is the night of the dear Savior's birth . . .
> A thrill of hope, a weary world rejoices,
> For yonder breaks a new and glorious morn.

Now the two high school students playing Mary and Joseph made their way to the altar. As they laid their precious bundle gently in the manger, angels and shepherds bowed their heads or knelt in homage. It was as if the Nativity story—one Nathan had heard so many times before—had come to life right before his eyes. And instead of being stale or phony, it somehow seemed new, exciting . . . *real.*

Nathan's notes seemed to grow stronger and stronger. He felt as though he were hearing the words of the old hymn for the first time.

Fall on your knees! Oh, hear the angel
voices!
O night divine!

When the song ended, he didn't know how
it had sounded to anyone else. The band may
have played off-key or been out of synch the
whole time. But Nathan had heard only hope
and joy and promise. No matter how it had
sounded, it had *felt* just right.

He had to hide his smile, though, when the
angels and shepherds left the altar to join their
families—Molly's halo had slipped from her
head and disappeared. Somehow that felt just
right, too.

Questions to Think and Talk About

O Holy Night

1. Have you ever felt resentful at having to change your own plans in order to help someone else, as Nathan did? How did you deal with those feelings?

2. At practice, Nathan gave his time—but not his best effort. How do you think his negative attitude may have affected others in the group?

3. During Mass, Nathan felt inspired by the Nativity play and the words of a sacred hymn. Have you ever felt closer to God when you saw or heard something beautiful?

4. Do you think some kids feel that Christmas is less important as they get older? How can we keep the joy of Christmas in our hearts at every age?

Secret Friends

By Diana R. Jenkins

"There's something on your locker, Zoe!" cried Midori.

When our school service club, Helping Hands, decided to do this secret friend thing for Christmas, I'd thought it was a dumb idea. Especially since that strange girl, Sadie, suggested it. But now that I had my first surprise, I was excited!

I quickly untied the gift bag from my locker handle and pulled out a can of salmon! "Aren't we supposed to give our secret friend nice things?"

"You like salmon," said Midori.

"But it's not a good Christmas surprise!" I opened my locker and stuck the can inside. "I *knew* this was a stupid idea."

Just then Sadie came along and shouted in her always-too-loud voice, "Hi! Get anything from your secret friend?"

"Yeah," I muttered. "Smelly old fish."

"Interesting," she said.

"We'd better get to math, Midori," I said, brushing past Sadie.

The next day, another bag appeared on my locker. Eagerly, I opened it and whipped out . . . "A bag of noodles?!"

"Letter noodles," Midori pointed out. "Remember how we used to spell out messages with this stuff?"

"I remember," I sighed, tossing the bag into my locker. "My secret friend sure isn't much of a friend. Like groceries are going to put me in the Christmas spirit!"

"Doesn't the spirit come from giving?" asked Midori.

"That reminds me! Look what I'm giving Amber." I showed her a teeny Christmas stocking. "See? I know how to be a good friend. Not like some people! I'm going to put this on her locker right now."

I was tying the stocking to Amber's locker handle when that doofus Sadie yelled in my ear, "Hi, Zoe! Is that for your secret friend?"

"No, I'm just decorating the lockers."

"HA, FUNNY!" bellowed Sadie.

"I have to go," I said, rolling my eyes and dashing off.

The next morning when I got to school, Midori was waiting at my locker. "Look! You got another surprise."

I opened the large bag in front of my locker and heaved out a jar of pickles!

"Those are your favorite!" said Midori.

"But they're not Christmassy." I pulled a stuffed angel out of my pack. "This is Christmassy! When Amber sees this, she'll think Christmas. She'll feel Christmas! And she'll be glad to have a secret Christmas friend like me. A real friend!" I held up the pickles.

"What kind of so-called friend gives pickles for Christmas?"

"It's the thought that counts," said Midori, sounding annoyed.

That's when I realized that *she* must be my secret friend! She knew how I liked salmon! And pickles! And what about our noodle messages?

Oh, no! I thought. *I've hurt her feelings!*

To make Midori feel better, I opened the jar and tasted a pickle. "Mmmm . . . delicious! Want one?"

She smiled and took a pickle. "So what if they're not Christmassy?"

"Hey, they're green," I said, closing the lid and setting the jar on my locker shelf.

At lunch, Sadie stopped by our table and boomed, "How are things going with your secret friend?"

I couldn't complain with Midori sitting right there. "Great!" I said in a happy-happy voice.

"Gee, who thought of such a great project?" Sadie snorted with laughter as she pulled out the chair beside me!

Thinking quickly, I told her, "That seat is saved."

"Oh," she said. "See you later."

The next day I gave Amber a Christmas bookmark, and Midori gave me a pen that wrote in purple ink. It was nice, but what's Christmassy about a purple ink pen?

After lunch on Friday, our last day as secret friends, I found another bag on my locker. I was hoping Midori finally left me something good, but the bag had three eggs inside! Which I'm allergic to! Which Midori knows!

"Is that from your secret friend?" Midori was standing beside me, looking into the bag and pretending to be puzzled.

Her other gifts were just lame. The eggs were out-and-out mean! What kind of friend does something like that?

I threw the bag into my locker, not caring whether the eggs were hard-boiled. "Leave me alone!" I snapped, slamming the door and walking away.

When I turned the corner, I ran right into Sadie. "Out of my way, dummy!" I yelled as I pushed her aside and stomped down the hall.

I avoided Midori all afternoon, but I had to see her at the Helping Hands party after school. I didn't have to sit by her, though! I sat with Amber, way in the back.

To start things off, our sponsor, Mrs. Windsor, called on people to guess who their secret friends were. Nobody could guess correctly.

When it was my turn, I confidently announced, "My secret friend is Midori."

"No, it's not," said Midori. "I would never give you eggs! I know you're allergic to them."

Sadie shrieked a window-rattling shriek. "You're allergic to eggs? Oh, no!"

It took a few seconds for the truth to sink in. "*You're* my secret friend?"

"I can't believe you didn't guess," she shouted. "I was afraid my clues were too obvious."

"Clues?"

"The gifts," she said. "Salmon, alphabet noodles, dill pickles, ink pen—"

"And eggs!" interrupted Midori. "I get it! Sadie was spelling out her name!" She looked at my confused face and added, "S for salmon, A for alphabet, D for dill . . . get it?"

"Yeah, I get it," I sighed.

"Sorry about the eggs," said Sadie, looking worried.

"That's okay," I said. "You didn't know."

"Who wants to guess next?" asked Mrs. Windsor.

I sat down with a heavy heart. How could I have suspected Midori of such a dirty trick? I felt like the worst friend in the world for doubting her!

Sadie was staring at me, still looking concerned. I was so mean to her, but she still cared about me! In fact, Sadie *tried* to be nice all along. (It wasn't like she meant to be annoying!) She even spent a lot of time figuring out a clever way to do her secret friend gifts. Sadie knew how to be a real friend—not like some people! (Okay . . . not like me! I had really messed up.)

While the guessing continued, I took a moment to ask God to help me make things right. *I want to be a good friend, Lord,* I told him.

Afterward, I felt better because I knew what I had to do. First, apologize to Midori and Sadie. Second, act like a real friend to both of them. (Even if Sadie and I never become best buddies!)

And third? I *had* to clean out my locker!

Questions to Think and Talk About

Secret Friends

1. What makes someone a real friend?

2. Zoe was unhappy because her gifts weren't what she expected. Have you ever felt disappointed at Christmas? Why?

3. God wants us to be kind to others, but sometimes that's difficult! What helps you keep your patience with annoying people?

4. Name some Christmas activities that are fun but inexpensive.

Lighting Up the Darkness

By Eugene M. Gagliano

Christmas was only a week away!

"Everybody's house is decorated except Mr. Weston's," said ten-year-old Jace.

"Well, remember how hard it was to get into the holiday spirit when Grandma died," Mom said.

Jace nodded. He'd never forget how sad he'd been two years ago.

"This is Mr. Weston's first Christmas without his wife," Mom added. "I've called him several times, but he just doesn't seem to feel like seeing anyone."

Maybe if . . . Jace thought.

He left the table and put on his winter jacket. Opening the refrigerator, he grabbed a carrot and stuck it into his pocket. He picked two prunes from a box on the counter and found a piece of red licorice in the cupboard. Rummaging through the hall closet, he unearthed an old baseball cap and a scarf that had seen better days. He pulled on his boots and gloves and hurried outside. Grabbing a snow shovel, he clattered down the front porch steps.

Jace walked to the end of the street, where Mr. Weston's dark house stood surrounded by a rickety picket fence. The curtains were drawn tight.

Quietly, Jace pushed open the sagging gate and quickly shoveled the front walk. Then he started rolling a snowman in the front yard. First the base—then the middle—and finally the head.

Finished! Jace plopped the baseball cap in place, then wrapped the tattered red plaid scarf around the snowman's neck. He poked in the two prunes for eyes and the carrot for a nose. Two small branches made fine arms.

Finally Jace used the red licorice to give his snowman a big, goofy grin. When Mr. Weston looked out his window, this was bound to cheer him up!

Back home, Jace peered through his bedroom blinds to see if Mr. Weston's curtains had parted, but the house remained closed up tight as a laced ice skate. Later, he saw the gray-bearded man slip out his door to check on the mail. He looked at the snowman for a moment, then shuffled to the mailbox, opened it, and snapped the empty container shut. Mr. Weston hurried back to the house without even another glance at the snowman. Jace sighed, but he had another idea.

"Mom, is it okay if I use one of the extra bows for a surprise?" Jace asked the next day.

"Of course," Mom said.

Jace tied the big bow on the post of his neighbor's mailbox. A bright red bow would certainly lift his spirits! But when Mr. Weston hobbled out of his house later, he didn't even seem to notice.

Christmas was fast approaching, and Mr. Weston still hadn't opened his curtains. What more could a kid do?

The next day, Jace asked Mom if he could take an old basket from the basement and fill it with treats for Mr. Weston. "What a great idea! Let's put in an invitation to Christmas dinner, too," Mom suggested.

Jace agreed. He picked some candy canes off the tree in the living room. After sampling one of Mom's sugar cookies (delicious!), he slid some into a plastic bag. He added a couple of bright red apples and some clementines from the bowl in the kitchen. Jace tucked in the invitation, tied on a bow, and hurried down the street. He carefully positioned the basket in front of the porch door, rang the doorbell, and hid behind a large spruce tree.

Mr. Weston opened the door and looked around. He picked up the basket and retreated into the house.

Jace hoped that Mr. Weston would open his curtains now to let in Christmas, but another day passed and nothing changed.

The day before Christmas Eve, Jace had one more idea. He walked to the Christmas tree lot three blocks away. "All Trees Half Price!" proclaimed a sign. Jace found a small fir tree he could afford with his allowance money, lugged it back, and left it on Mr. Weston's front porch.

This would do the trick for sure! Back home, Jace waited for the old man to get his mail. When Mr. Weston saw the tree, he'd just have to take it inside and decorate it and finally feel the holiday spirit. But when Mr. Weston picked up the mail, he studied the tree for a long time and then hurried inside without it.

Jace sighed. Would the spirit of Christmas ever warm the old man's sad heart?

On Christmas Eve, Jace went caroling with his church group to Mr. Weston's house. The moonlit night was Minnesota-frosty as the carolers sang "Silent Night" in front of the dark house. As the last notes died away, Jace noticed the living room curtains part. There was the little Christmas tree, glowing with red, yellow, and green lights. The front door creaked open, and Mr. Weston appeared.

"See you at dinner tomorrow, Jace," he said with a smile. "It's finally Christmas!"

Questions to Think and Talk About

Lighting Up the Darkness

1. What did Jace do to help Mr. Weston get into the Christmas spirit? What else could Jace have done to brighten Mr. Weston's spirit?

2. Why do you think Jace wanted to help Mr. Weston?

3. How could Jace help Mr. Weston during the new year?

4. Who could you help this Christmas? How?

Thanks a Million!

By Diana R. Jenkins

"Anna is so rude," I told Cher as we left class and headed for our lockers. "I helped her pick up these colored pencils she dropped, and you know what she said?"

"What?" asked Cher.

I grabbed my stuff and slammed the locker shut. "Nothing! Not one word of thanks!"

"But, Tori," said Cher, "she might have—"

The warning bell drowned her words. "Rats! I don't have time to go to the library. Could you return this on your way to PE?" I handed her a book. "Thanks a million!"

"I don't have much time either," said Cher.

"You can take the back hall and go right by. Thanks!" I hurried off toward math class.

I forgot Anna's rudeness until she showed up for the after-school meeting about the Christmas food drive. I was running the drive, so I was glad to see so many volunteers. But I wasn't happy when Anna sailed past me as I held the library door open. Once again, she didn't say thanks!

When I got inside, I quickly started the meeting—which didn't take long. First, I passed out a sign-up sheet. Then I explained how one person from each home room should take an empty box from the stack in the corner to use for their food collection. "Please decorate your boxes and make them look Christmassy," I said politely. "You know . . . wrapping paper . . . bows . . . stickers. And have them in place by Monday. Then talk to your class about what they should bring. Here's a list of suggested ideas."

I handed Cher the stack of lists. "Could you pass these out? Thanks!" Hey, *I* had good manners!

"Stay after every Friday this month and bring your food here," I went on. "We'll sort it and put it in the storeroom. The people from the food bank will pick it up the Friday before Christmas. That's it!" I took the sign-up sheet from the last person. "Thanks a million!"

People were already on their feet when Anna said, "Wait! What if we have questions?"

"Like what?" I asked.

"We-e-ell," she said while everybody just stood there. "Like . . . I don't know . . ."

"Okay then!" I said. "I'll see everybody on Friday."

After everyone left, I told Cher about Anna's rudeness at the door. "And why was she making everybody hang around when she didn't actually have a question?"

"I guess she couldn't think that fast," said Cher.

"But we were supposed to wait anyway. How thoughtless was that?" I grabbed a box for our home room. "Hey, could you decorate this?"

"I'm pretty busy," said Cher. "The choir is practicing a lot for the program and I—"

"But you're creative, so you should do it." I gave her the box. "Thanks!"

Before the next meeting, Cher and I put signs on the library tables to make it easy to organize the food into vegetables, meats, and other categories. When people came in with their boxes, we quickly sorted the food, bagged it, and put it in the storeroom. We were finished in no time!

"Take your collection boxes back to your rooms," I said. "See you next Friday. Thanks so much!"

As people left, Anna practically knocked me over with her box. "Excuse you!" I called after her.

She turned back. "What?"

I didn't want to be rude, too, so I said, "Thanks for helping out, Anna. Really. Thanks a million."

She frowned and said, "Whatever." Then she walked out.

I turned to Cher, who was collecting the signs. "She has no manners at all."

"Having manners isn't just saying the right words, Tori," she said. "Being thoughtful means more than that."

"I know!" I said. "Hey, thanks for making the signs," I added thoughtfully.

Some people didn't show up for the next meeting, so I sent a few of the others to get their boxes. I made sure to thank them, of course. "And could you guys please hurry? We don't have all day." But by the time they returned, all the other food was in the storeroom and most people had already gone.

"Can you stay and help sort this stuff?" I asked Cher and Anna and the few people who were still there.

"My mom's waiting outside," said Anna. Then she walked out!

Those of us who were left started sorting the rest of the donations. As Cher and I bagged some boxed foods, I said, "Anna is the most thoughtless person I ever met! She doesn't have any manners. She doesn't care about anybody else. She—"

"You must be joking!" said an angry voice from behind me.

I turned to see Anna standing right there! "I . . . uh . . ."

"I don't care?" cried Anna. "When you wanted me to stay, I went right out and asked my mom if it was okay."

"Yeah, but—"

"And you think I'm thoughtless?" she interrupted again. "You order people around like you're the boss of the world, but that's okay since you always say thank you, right?" Her voice cracked, and she ran out of the library.

Everybody was staring, but they went back to work when I looked their way.

"How awful!" Cher whispered.

"See? I was right about her," I said.

Cher gave me a strange look. "I meant how awful for Anna. You hurt her feelings."

"Well, she shouldn't have been eaves-dropping. It's rude!"

Cher slammed a box of rice onto the table. "Anna is right about you. You're the one who's thoughtless." She started to leave but turned back. "Don't bother to thank me, okay?" Then she stomped out!

I pretended everything was fine while the rest of us finished, but inside I was furious. How could Cher say that about me? I was running a food drive so needy people wouldn't go hungry at Christmas! That was incredibly thoughtful!

It didn't take long to sort the rest of the food. When the others started to leave, I thanked them. Like always! *I am thoughtful!* I told myself. *I am!*

On my way out, I saw Anna leave the bathroom, wiping her eyes. I could see I had really hurt her feelings! She glared at me and walked away. I was going to just let her go, but then I realized something. A thoughtful person would try to make things right with her.

Maybe I hadn't been that kind of person so far—hey, Cher wouldn't lie to me!—but I could change. I caught up with Anna and apologized big-time for my thoughtlessness. Then I asked, "Could you give me another chance?"

Anna smiled and said, "Okay."

"Thanks a million!" I said in my usual way. Then I added, "I mean . . . thanks."

I said it like it really meant something. Because now it did!

Questions to Think and Talk About

Thanks a Million!

1. During the holidays, there are many helpful programs like food drives. How can we help others throughout the year?

2. Why are good manners important?

3. Was Tori a good leader? Why or why not?

4. What can you do to be more thoughtful?

The Day of the Three Kings

By Kathleen M. Muldoon

Noreen shivered as she sat on the steps of Grandma Murphy's house. It was January 5, and she noticed that most neighbors had taken down their Christmas decorations—all except the people across the street. Lights twinkled on their roof, in their windows, and on their fence.

Noreen had spent Christmas with Grandma, whose house had no Christmas lights—but did have iron bars covering every window. *Just like a prison,* Noreen thought.

A wind gust made her snuggle deeper into her coat. Still, she'd rather be outside than inside, helping Grandma sort yarn for the afghans she knitted. Noreen sighed. She wished Mom and Dad weren't away taking care of Nana Parker. But mostly she wished Grandma was jolly, like the grandmother across the street whom she'd heard the children call "Abuela."

Today as Noreen watched, the boy and girl lined up shoes on the porch. Then they brought out a pail of water and a bundle of straw. *What ARE they doing?* Noreen wondered. Just then the girl waved. As Noreen smiled and waved back, Grandma opened the door.

"Come inside," she said. "It's cold out there."

After supper, while Noreen helped Grandma wind yellow yarn into balls, she told her about the strange things on the porch across the street.

"This used to be a friendly neighborhood," Grandma said. "Now everything is different. I don't know the people who live around here anymore."

"Why not, Grandma?"

"Because you can't talk to them" Grandma said. "So many are from other countries. They don't understand our ways."

Noreen frowned. "But can't you get to know them?"

Before Grandma could answer, the doorbell rang. Grandma tiptoed to the door. Noreen followed. She peeked through the side window. On the porch stood Abuela and the children from across the street. Grandma opened the door a crack.

Noreen heard Abuela say something in Spanish. Then the girl spoke.

"I'm Perla, and this is my brother, Pedro, and my *abuela*," she said. "Abuela wants you to come tomorrow for *El Dia de los Tres Reyes*."

Noreen squeezed in front of Grandma and opened the door all the way.

"I'm Noreen," she said. "I'm visiting my grandmother. What is . . . what is that thing you said?"

Pedro grinned. "The Day of the Kings. We remember the day the three kings visited Baby Jesus. We leave hay and water for their camels. And tonight while we sleep, the kings fill our shoes with candies and toys!"

"Abuela is teaching us how they celebrate in Mexico," Perla added.

Abuela smiled and nodded at Grandma.

"Come," she said in a musical voice. "Eat with us. Bring the girl."

She reached out to squeeze Grandma Murphy's hand, then turned to walk back across the street.

"Please, Grandma," Noreen begged after they'd closed the door. "It'll be fun."

"I don't know," Grandma said.

The next day, Grandma reluctantly agreed to go.

"I don't know what to wear," she complained.

First she put on a blue dress and then changed to a green one.

"Wear your purple dress," Noreen said. "That's the royal color that kings and queens wear."

Noreen put on the pink dress Mom and Dad had sent her for Christmas. She tied her hair with a matching ribbon and then tied another around Grandma's gray braid.

"Maybe we should have lunch before we go," Grandma said. "No telling what they'll give us to eat."

"Grandma!" Noreen said. "Their feelings will be hurt if we don't eat their food. It'll be an adventure!"

Finally they stepped out onto the porch, but Grandma turned back. Before Noreen could follow, Grandma returned with a purple and gold afghan.

"We should bring something," she said.

Abuela answered their knock on the door. She threw her arms around Grandma and Noreen. She hugged the purple and gold afghan.

"*Graciás!* Thank you! *Que bonita!* How beautiful!"

Abuela introduced them to Perla and Pedro's parents, Señor and Señora Ramos. They met aunts, uncles, cousins, three dogs, and two cats. Music, laughter, and wonderful smells filled the air.

Soon Grandma was talking to Abuela and two aunts about making afghans. Noreen and the other children followed Señor Ramos outside. A crown-shaped piñata swung from a tree in the back yard.

"It's filled with candy and surprises," Pedro told Noreen.

They took turns wearing a blindfold and hitting the piñata with a stick. Everyone giggled and screeched, especially when Noreen missed the piñata altogether. Finally Pedro broke it open with a mighty WHACK. Candies and toys tumbled to the ground. With whoops and hollers, the children gathered the treasures.

"Look!" Noreen told Perla. "I got a bracelet with beads the color of my dress."

"It's time!" Señora Ramos called from the porch.

"Time for what?" Noreen asked.

But the others were already running to the house. Noreen raced behind them. Soon they were all squeezed around the dining room table. Señora Ramos served steaming cups of hot chocolate. Then Abuela carried in a ring of golden bread. To Noreen it looked like a crown.

Cherries on the sides of the bread shone like jewels.

"It's beautiful!" Grandma exclaimed.

"It's *rosca de reyes*," said Perla. "Three kings' bread. It's yummy, but that's not all! Tell them, Abuela."

"Something special is inside," Abuela said slowly. "*El niño*—a tiny baby—is baked in the bread."

"We each cut a piece," Pedro interrupted, bouncing up and down. "Whoever gets the Baby Jesus doll in their piece . . . I forget. What happens, Abuela?"

"Wait and see," she answered, her eyes twinkling.

Noreen held her breath as two aunts, an uncle, and two cousins cut their pieces of bread. Finally her turn came. Carefully, she cut her piece and put it on the plate. She stuck a fork through it but found no doll.

Suddenly cheers filled the room as Grandma held up a plastic baby doll.

"Do I get a prize?" she asked.

The women at the table laughed and poked each other.

"Tell her," Abuela said to Señora Ramos.

"Well, Abuela Murphy," Señora Ramos said, "you get to make the *tamales* and *atole* for *Dia de Candelaria*!"

"Oh, my!" Grandma sputtered. "I don't even know what that is!"

"Another fiesta. I will help," Abuela promised. "We have four weeks to get ready."

Grandma groaned, but Noreen had never seen her look happier. All too soon it was time to leave. Abuela gave them a sack of food to bring home.

"Grandma," said Noreen when they reached their porch, "Don't you think I'd better stay with you for *Dia de Candelaria*?"

"You'd better," Grandma said. "First we have to find out what it is!"

Noreen peeked at the lights across the street. *Maybe we can have the fiesta here,* she thought. She closed her eyes and imagined twinkling

lights on the roof and in the windows and all
around the fence of Grandma Murphy's yard.
Smiling, she shut the door. . . for now.

Questions to Think and Talk About

The Day of the Three Kings

1. Why do you think that gift-giving is part of the Day of the Kings celebration?

2. Noreen and Grandma Murphy had to learn to taste new foods and celebrate a new holiday. Does it make you nervous to try new things? What can you do to get over your fears?

3. Is it important to share our traditions with people of other cultures?

4. Do you think Grandma Murphy will visit her neighbors after Noreen goes back home to her parents? Why or why not?

Anna Mei, Cartoon Girl

By Carol A. Grund

No matter what her name sounds like, Anna Mei is *not* a cartoon character. But she *is* the new kid at school, and that just wasn't in the plan.

How's she ever going to fit in with the other sixth graders when she has a weird name, an adoptive family she doesn't remotely resemble, and an unknown birth mother somewhere back in China? She figures she'd better get busy transforming herself into someone who's less . . . unusual. After all, a pretend life is better than no life. But just when it looks as though Anna Mei 2.0 has everyone fooled, a school project comes along that makes her think about herself, her friends, her family—and that weird name of hers—in a whole new way.

Paperback
144 pp.
07885
$8.95 U.S.

The
Stepping Stones Journals

By Diana R. Jenkins

Alberto, Chantal, Denver, and Suki are back, but this time your friends from the popular *Stepping Stones* comics share their personal journals! In *The Stepping Stones Journals*, all four tell about the ups and downs of their lives in their own words—and you get to experience it firsthand. Like you, the *Stepping Stones* kids are dealing with family and friends, school and church, decisions and challenges. So follow along as they travel the stepping stones of life and journey toward a closer relationship to God!

Paperback, 144 pp.
7129X $8.95 U.S.

Stepping Stones:
The Comic Collection

Paperback, 128 pp.
71184 $9.95 U.S.

Who are the Daughters of St. Paul?

We are Catholic sisters. Our mission is to be like Saint Paul and tell everyone about Jesus! There are so many ways for people to communicate with each other. We want to use all of them so everyone will know how much God loves us. We do this by printing books (you're holding one!), making radio shows, singing, helping people at our bookstores, using the Internet, and in many other ways.

Visit our Web site at www.pauline.org

BOOKS & MEDIA

The Daughters of St. Paul operate book and media centers at the following addresses. Visit, call or write the one nearest you today, or find us on the World Wide Web, www.pauline.org

CALIFORNIA
3908 Sepulveda Blvd, Culver City, CA 90230   310-397-8676
2640 Broadway Street, Redwood City, CA 94063   650-369-4230
5945 Balboa Avenue, San Diego, CA 92111   858-565-9181

FLORIDA
145 S.W. 107th Avenue, Miami, FL 33174   305-559-6715

HAWAII
1143 Bishop Street, Honolulu, HI 96813   808-521-2731

Neighbor Islands call: 866-521-2731

ILLINOIS
172 North Michigan Avenue, Chicago, IL 60601   312-346-4228

LOUISIANA
4403 Veterans Memorial Blvd, Metairie, LA 70006   504-887-7631

MASSACHUSETTS
885 Providence Hwy, Dedham, MA 02026   781-326-5385

MISSOURI
9804 Watson Road, St. Louis, MO 63126   314-965-3512

NEW YORK
64 West 38th Street, New York, NY 10018   212-754-1110

PENNSYLVANIA
Philadelphia—relocating   215-969-5068

SOUTH CAROLINA
243 King Street, Charleston, SC 29401   843-577-0175

VIRGINIA
1025 King Street, Alexandria, VA 22314   703-549-3806

CANADA
3022 Dufferin Street, Toronto, ON M6B 3T5   416-781-9131